MW01599017

POETRY FOR CHILDREN

Oliphaunt

By J. R. R. Tolkien
Illustrated by Dan McGeehan

Distributed by The Child's World®
1980 Lookout Drive • Mankato, MN 56003-1705
800-599-READ • www.childsworld.com

Acknowledgments
The Child's World®: Mary Berendes, Publishing Director
The Design Lab: Kathleen Petelinsek, Design

Library of Congress Cataloging-in-Publication Data
Tolkien, J. R. R. (John Ronald Reuel), 1892–1973.
  Oliphaunt / by J.R.R. Tolkien ; illustrated by Dan McGeehan.
    p. cm.
  ISBN 978-1-60973-155-7 (library reinforced : alk. paper)
  1. Elephants—Juvenile poetry. 2. Children's poetry, English. I. McGeehan, Dan, ill.
II. Title.
  PR6039.O32.O4 2011
  821'.912—dc22   2011005001

Printed in the United States of America in Mankato, Minnesota.
July 2011
PA02091

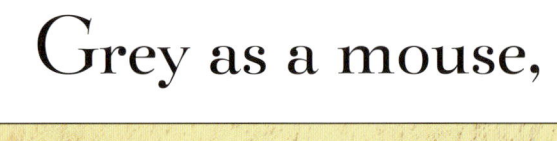

Grey as a mouse,

big as a house,

nose like a snake,

I make the earth shake.
As I tramp through the grass;
trees crack as I pass.

With horns in my mouth,
I walk in the South,
flapping big ears.

Beyond count of years
I stump round and round,
never lie on the ground,
not even to die.

Oliphaunt am I . . .

biggest of all,
huge, old, and tall.

If ever you'd met me,
you wouldn't forget me.

If you never do,
you won't think I'm true;
But old Oliphaunt am I,
and I never lie.